THIS WALKER BOOK BELONGS TO:

_____

_____

_____

For Graham,
Katy and Lauren

First published 1997 by Walker Books Ltd
87 Vauxhall Walk, London SE11 5HJ

This edition published 2005

4 6 8 10 9 7 5 3

© 1997 Jez Alborough

The right of Jez Alborough to be identified as author/
illustrator of this work has been asserted by him in accordance
with the Copyright, Designs and Patents Act 1988

This book has been typeset in Usherwood Bold

Printed in China

British Library Cataloguing in Publication Data:
a catalogue record for this book is available
from the British Library

ISBN 978-0-7445-9834-6

www.walker.co.uk

# WATCH OUT! BIG BRO'S COMING!

## Jez Alborough

WALKER BOOKS

AND SUBSIDIARIES

LONDON · BOSTON · SYDNEY · AUCKLAND

"Help!" squeaked a mouse.
  "He's coming!"

"Who's coming?" asked a frog.

"Big Bro," said the mouse.
  "He's rough, he's tough, and he's big."

"Big?" said the frog. "How big?"

The mouse stretched out his arms
  as wide as they could go.

"This big," he cried,
and he scampered off to hide.

"Look out!" croaked the frog.
    "Big Bro's coming!"

"Big who?" asked the parrot.

"Big Bro," said the frog. "He's rough,
    he's tough, and he's really big."

"Really big?" said the parrot. "How big?"

The frog
stretched out his arms
as wide as they could go.
"This big," he cried,
    and he hopped off
        to hide.

"Watch out!" squawked the parrot.
"Big Bro's coming!"

"Who's he?"
asked the chimpanzee.

"Don't you know Big Bro?"
asked the parrot. "He's rough,
he's tough, and he's ever so big."

"Ever so big?" said the chimpanzee.
"How big?"

The parrot stretched out his wings
as wide as they could go.
"This big," he cried,
and he flapped off
to hide.

"Ooh-ooh! Look out!"
whooped the chimpanzee.
"Big Bro's coming!"

"Big Joe?" said the elephant.

"No," said the chimpanzee. "Big Bro.
He's rough, he's tough, and everybody
knows how big Big Bro is."

The elephant shook his head.
"I don't," he said.

The chimpanzee stretched out
his arms as wide as they could go.
"This big," he cried.

"That big?" gulped the elephant.
"Let's hide!"

So there they all were, hiding
and waiting, waiting and hiding.

"Where is he?"
asked the elephant.

"Shhh," said the chimpanzee.
"I don't know."

"Why don't you creep out
and have a look around?"
whispered the elephant.

"Not me,"
  said the chimpanzee.

"Not me,"
  said the parrot.

"Not me,"
  said the frog.

"All right," said the mouse.
  "As you're all so
  frightened, I'll go."

The mouse tiptoed
ever so slowly
out from his
hiding place.

He looked this way
and that way
to see if he could
see Big Bro.

And then...
"He's coming!"
shrieked
the mouse.

"H ...
h ...
h ...
hide!"

Big Bro came closer
and closer and closer.
Everyone covered their eyes.

"Oh no," whispered the frog.

"Help," gasped the parrot.

"I can hear something coming,"
whined the chimpanzee.

"It's him," whimpered
the elephant.
*"It's ... it's ..."*

# "BIG BRO!"

shrieked the mouse.

"Is that Big Bro?" asked the frog.

"He's tiny," said the parrot.

"Teeny weeny," said the chimpanzee.

"He's a mouse," said the elephant.

Big Bro looked up at them all,
took a deep breath,
and said …

"Come on, Little Bro," said Big Bro. "Mum wants you back home *now*!"

"Wow," said the elephant.

"Phew," said the chimpanzee.

"He is rough," said the parrot.

"And tough," said the frog.

"Rough and tough," said Little Bro, looking back over his shoulder.

"And I *told* you he was big!"

WALKER BOOKS is the world's leading
independent publisher of children's books.
Working with the best authors and illustrators
we create books for all ages, from babies
to teenagers – books your child will
grow up with and always remember. So…

FOR THE BEST CHILDREN'S BOOKS,
LOOK FOR THE BEAR